D0574390

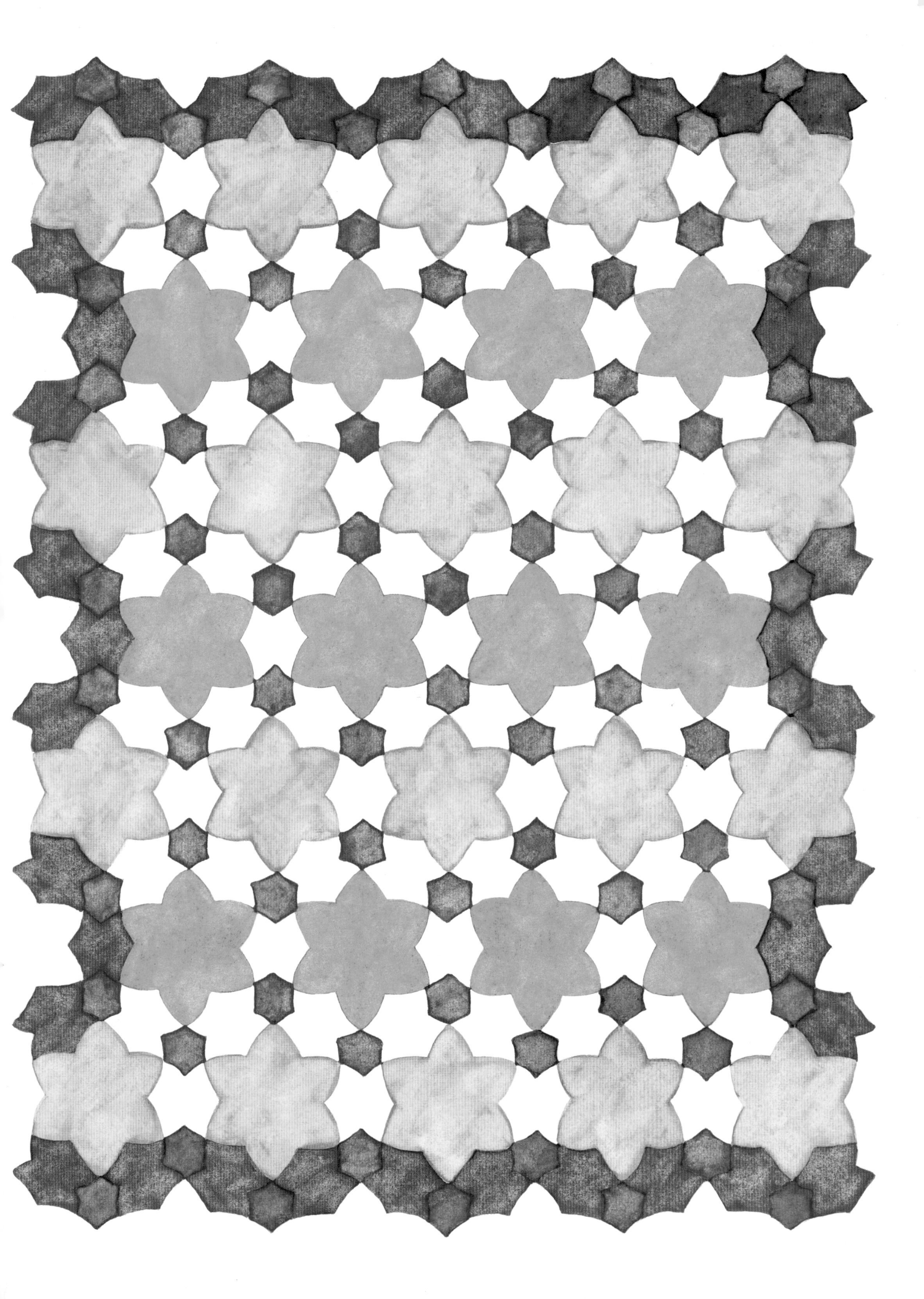

First Edition 1998
Second Impression 2001
Third Impression 2005

Published by Hoopoe Books
a division of The Institute for the Study of Human Knowledge

The original version of *The Magic Horse* was published in 1968
in *Caravan of Dreams* by Idries Shah,
published by The Octagon Press Ltd., London.

ISBN: 1-883536-11-1
Library of Congress Cataloging-in-Publication Data

Shah, Idries, 1924-
The magic horse / by Idries Shah; illustrated by Julie Freeman.
p. cm.
Summary: A teaching tale in which two very different princes find their hearts' desires: one in a wondrous, mechanical fish, the other in a magical wooden horse.
ISBN 1-883536-11-1 (hdbk.)
[1. Folklore.} I. Freeman, Julie, ill. II. Title.
PZ8.1.S47Mag 1997
[398.22]–dc21
97-5086
CIP
AC

The Magic Horse

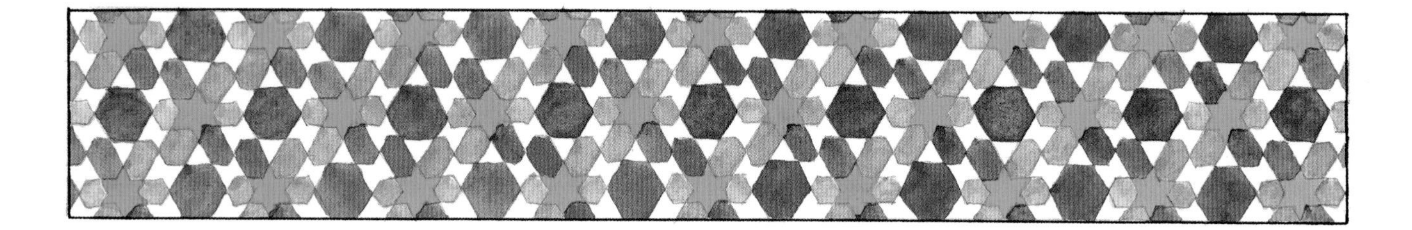

THE TEACHING STORY

The Magic Horse is one of the hundreds of stories collected by Idries Shah.

In the Sufi tradition there is a continuum between the children's story, the entertainment or folklore story, and the instructional or instrumental story. A story can help children deal with difficult situations and give them something to hold on to. It can, at the same time, stimulate a deeper understanding in adults.

Through the instrumental function of this rich body of oral and written material, we and our children can now learn to develop the capacity to be more flexible and to understand many more things about ourselves and about life.

The
Magic Horse
Written by Idries Shah
Illustrated by Julie Freeman

Once upon a time - not so very long ago - there was a land in which the people were very prosperous. They had made all kinds of discoveries in the growing of plants, in harvesting and preserving fruits, in making objects for sale to other countries, and in many other practical arts.

Their ruler was unusually enlightened, and he encouraged new discoveries and activities because he knew they would help his people.

He had two sons, Tambal and Hoshyar. Hoshyar was expert in using strange devices. Tambal was a dreamer who seemed interested only in things which were of little value in the eyes of the citizens.

From time to time the king, whose name was King Mumkin, would make this announcement:

"Let all those who have interesting and useful devices present them to the palace for examination so that they may be rewarded."

Now there were two men of that country, an ironsmith and a woodworker, who were great rivals in most things, and each delighted in making strange contraptions. When they heard this announcement one day, they agreed to compete for an award so that their relative merits could be decided once and for all, and recognized in public by the king.

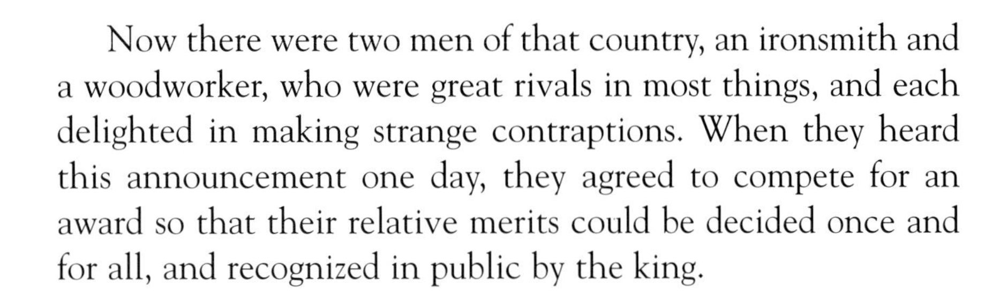

The ironsmith worked day and night on a mighty engine with the help of many talented specialists. And he surrounded his workshop with high walls to keep his work secret.

The woodworker took his simple tools and went into a forest where, after long and solitary reflection, he prepared his own masterpiece.

News of the rivalry spread, and people thought that the ironsmith would easily win, for his cunning works had been seen before, and while the woodworker's products were admired, they were not very useful.

When both were ready, the king received them in court.

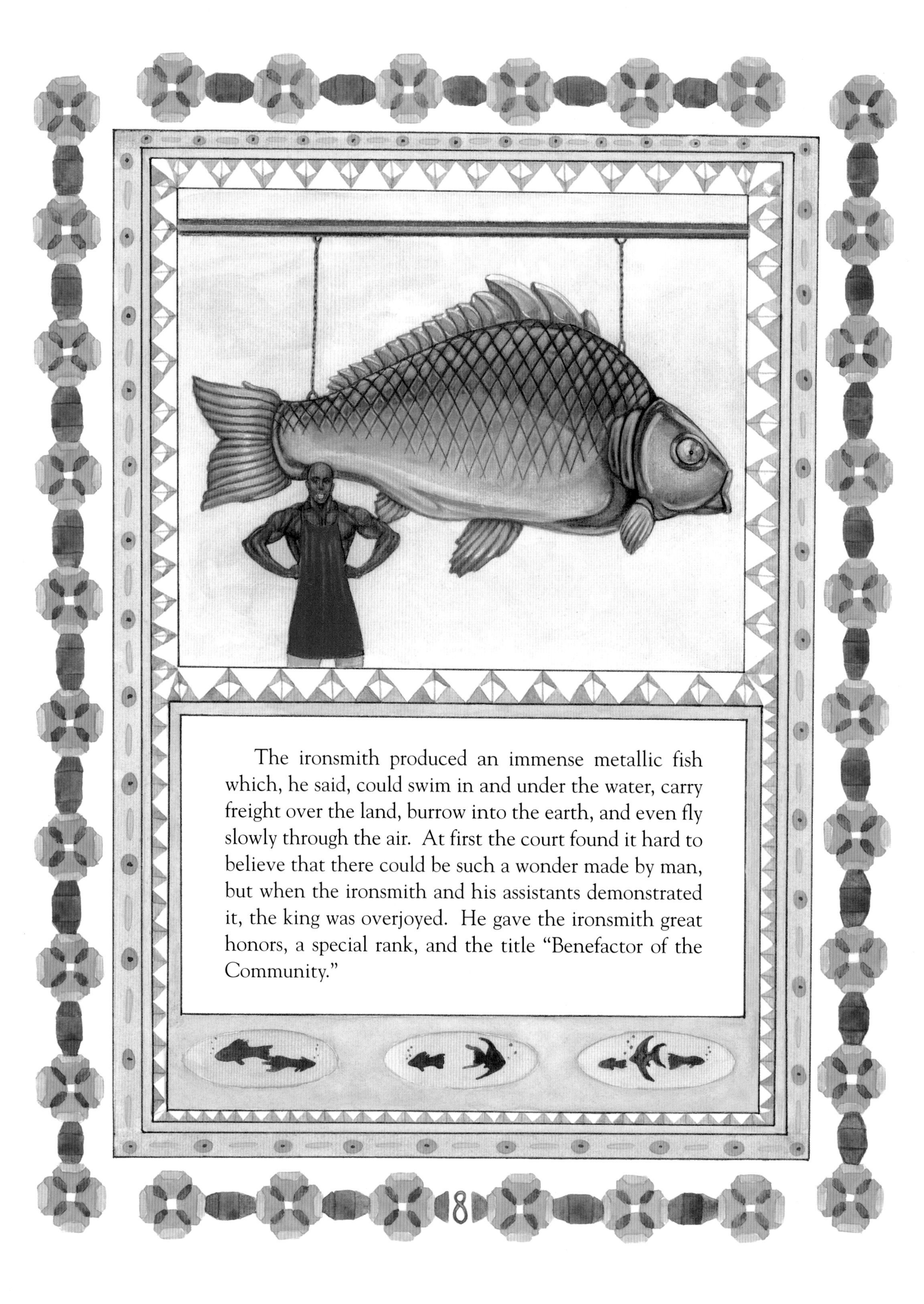

The ironsmith produced an immense metallic fish which, he said, could swim in and under the water, carry freight over the land, burrow into the earth, and even fly slowly through the air. At first the court found it hard to believe that there could be such a wonder made by man, but when the ironsmith and his assistants demonstrated it, the king was overjoyed. He gave the ironsmith great honors, a special rank, and the title "Benefactor of the Community."

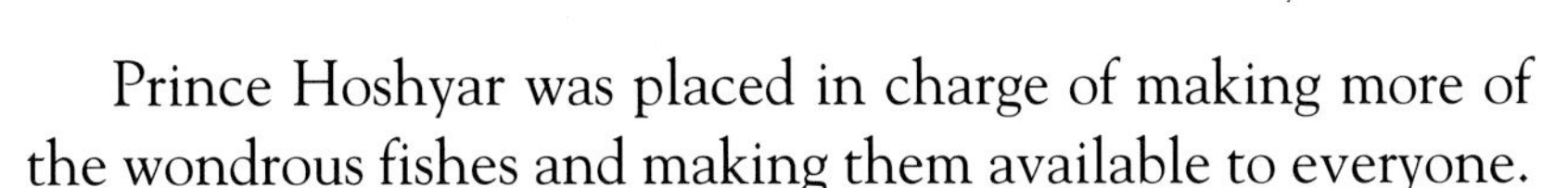

Prince Hoshyar was placed in charge of making more of the wondrous fishes and making them available to everyone.

The people blessed the ironsmith and Hoshyar, as well as the kind and wise monarch whom they loved so much.

In the excitement, the humble carpenter had been all but forgotten. Then one day someone said, "But what about the contest? Where is the entry of the woodworker? We all know him to be a clever man. Perhaps he has produced something useful."

"How could anything be as useful as the wondrous fishes?" asked Hoshyar. And many of the people agreed with him.

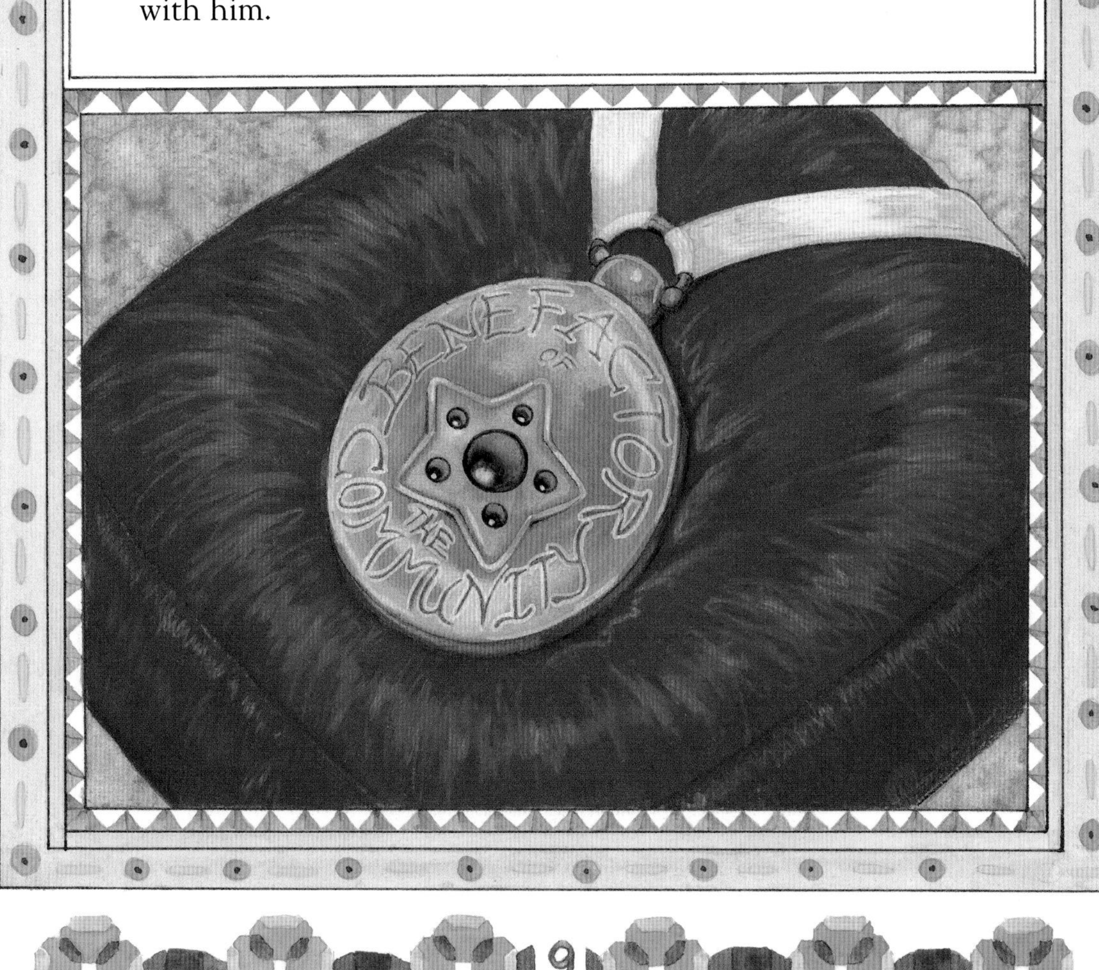

But one day the king was bored. He had grown tired of the fishes and the reports of their wonders which they so regularly performed. He said, "Call the woodcarver, for I would now like to see what he has made."

The simple woodcarver came into the throne-room, carrying a parcel wrapped in coarse cloth. As the whole court craned forward to see what he had, he took off the covering to reveal - a wooden horse. It was beautifully carved and decorated with colored paints, but the king snapped, "It's a mere plaything!"

"But, Father," said Prince Tambal, "let us ask the man what it is for."

"Very well," said the king. "What is it for?"

"Your Majesty," stammered the woodcarver, "it is a magic horse. It does not look impressive, but it has its own inner senses. Unlike the fish, which has to be directed, this horse can interpret the desires of the rider and carry him wherever he needs to go."

"Such a silly thing is fit only for Tambal," murmured the chief minister at the king's elbow. "It cannot compare to the wondrous fish."

The woodcarver was preparing sadly to depart when Tambal said, "Father, let me have the wooden horse."

"All right," said the king, "give it to him. Take the woodcarver away and tie him to a tree so that he will realize that our time is valuable. Let him think about how rich the wondrous fish has made us, and perhaps when he has had time to think about how to really work, we shall let him go free to practice what he has learnt."

The woodcarver was taken away, and Prince Tambal left the court carrying the magic horse.

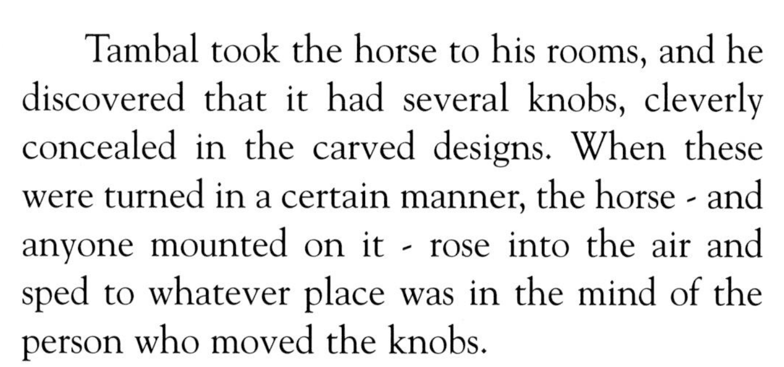

Tambal took the horse to his rooms, and he discovered that it had several knobs, cleverly concealed in the carved designs. When these were turned in a certain manner, the horse - and anyone mounted on it - rose into the air and sped to whatever place was in the mind of the person who moved the knobs.

In this way, day after day, Tambal flew to places he had never visited before, and he came to know a great many things. He took the horse with him everywhere.

One day he met Hoshyar, who said to him, “Carrying a wooden horse is just the thing for someone like you. As for me, I am working for the good of all, towards my heart’s desire!”

Tambal thought, “I wish I knew what the good of all is. And I wish I could know what my heart’s desire is.”

When he was next in his room, he sat upon the horse, turned the knobs, and thought, “I would like to find my heart’s desire.”

More swiftly than light, the horse rose into the air and carried the prince a thousand ordinary days away to a far kingdom that was ruled by a magician-king.

The king, whose name was Kahana, had a beautiful daughter called Precious Pearl. In order to protect her, he had imprisoned her in a palace that wheeled in the sky, higher than any mortal could reach. As Tambal was approaching the magic land, he saw the glittering palace in the heavens, and he alighted there.

The princess and the young horseman met and fell in love.

"My father will never allow us to marry," she said, "for he has commanded that I must marry the son of another magician-king who lives across the cold desert to the east of our homeland. He wants to unify the two kingdoms by this marriage, and no one dares to disobey him."

"I will go to him and try to reason with him," said Tambal, mounting the magic horse.

But when he descended into the magic land, there were so many new and exciting things to see that he did not hurry to the palace. When he finally arrived, the drum at the gate was beating, which meant that the king was absent. Tambal asked when the king would return.

"He has gone to visit his daughter in the Whirling Palace," said a man on the street, "and he usually spends several hours with her."

Tambal went to a quiet place where he willed the horse to carry him to the king's private apartment. "I will approach him in his own home," he thought to himself, "for if I go to the Whirling Palace without his permission, he may be angry."

When he got to the king's apartment, he hid behind some curtains and lay down to sleep.

Meanwhile, unable to keep her secret, Princess Precious Pearl had confessed to her father that a man on a flying horse had visited her and wanted to marry her. King Kahana was furious.

He placed sentries around the Whirling Palace and returned to his own apartment to think things over. As soon as he entered his bedchamber, one of his tongueless magic servants guarding it pointed to the wooden horse lying in a corner. "Aha!" exclaimed the magician-king. "Now I have him. Let us look at this horse and see what manner of thing it may be."

As he and his servants were examining the horse, the prince slipped away and hid in another part of the palace.

The king twisted the knobs, tapped the horse, and tried to understand how it worked, but he was baffled. "Take that thing away," he said. "It has no use now, if it ever had any. It is just a toy, fit only for children."

And so the horse was put into a cupboard.

Now King Kahana thought that he should arrange his daughter's wedding without delay in case the man with the horse had other ways to win her. So he called her to his palace and sent a message to the other magician-king, whose son was to marry Princess Precious Pearl, asking that the prince be sent to claim his bride.

Meanwhile, Prince Tambal escaped from the palace when the guards were asleep and decided to return to his own country. His quest for his heart's desire now seemed almost hopeless, but he said to himself, "If it takes the rest of my life, I shall return with troops to take this kingdom by force. I can do that only by convincing my father that I must have his help to attain my heart's desire."

So saying, he set off. Never was a man worse equipped for such a journey. An alien, traveling on foot, without any kind of provisions, facing pitiless heat, freezing nights, and sandstorms, he soon became hopelessly lost in the desert.

Delirious, Tambal blamed himself, his father, the magician-king, the woodcarver, even the princess and the magic horse itself. Sometimes he thought he saw water ahead of him, sometimes fair cities. Sometimes he felt elated, sometimes incomparably sad.

Sometimes he thought he had companions in his difficulties, but when he shook himself he saw that he was quite alone.

He felt that he had been traveling for an eternity. Suddenly, when he had given up and started again several times, he saw something right in front of him that at first looked like a mirage. It was a garden full of delicious fruits that sparkled and beckoned him to come closer.

At first Tambal did not take much notice and continued walking, but soon he realized that he was passing through such a garden.

He gathered some of the fruits and tasted them cautiously. They were delicious. They took away his fear as well as his hunger and thirst. When he was full, he lay down in the shade of a huge, welcoming tree and fell asleep.

When he woke up he felt well enough, but something seemed to be wrong. Running to a nearby pool, he looked at his reflection in the water. Staring up at him was a horrible sight. He saw a long beard, curved horns, and ears a foot long. He looked down at his hands. They were covered with fur.

Was it a nightmare? Pinching and beating himself, he tried to wake up. But it was no use. Beside himself with fear and horror, screaming and sobbing, he threw himself on the ground. "Whether I live or die," he thought, "these fruits have ruined me. Even with the greatest army of all time, conquest will not help me. Nobody would marry me now, especially not Princess Precious Pearl. Even beasts would be terrified at the sight of me, and my heart's desire would surely reject me!" And he lost consciousness.

When he woke again, in the dark, he saw a light approaching through the groves of silent trees. Fear and hope struggled in him. As the light came closer, he saw that it was a lamp enclosed in a brilliant starlike shape. The lamp was carried by a bearded man who walked in the pool of brightness that it cast around.

"My son," said the man to Tambal, "you have been affected by the influences of this place. If I had not come along, you would have remained just another beast of this enchanted grove, for there are many more like you. But I can help you."

Tambal wondered whether this man was a fiend in disguise, perhaps the very owner of the evil trees. But, as his sense returned, he realized that he had nothing to lose.

"Help me, Father," he said.

"If you really want your heart's desire," said the wise man, "you have only to fix this desire firmly in your mind, not thinking of the fresh, delicious fruit. You must then take up some of the dried fruits that are lying at the foot of all these trees and eat them. Then follow your destiny."

So saying, he walked away.

As the sage's light disappeared into the darkness, Tambal saw that the moon was rising, and in its pale light he could see that there were indeed piles of dried fruits under every tree.

He gathered some and ate them as quickly as he could.

Slowly the fur disappeared from his hands and arms. The horns shrank, then vanished. The beard fell away. He was himself again.

By now it was first light, and in the dawn he heard the tinkling of camel bells. A grand procession was coming through the enchanted forest.

As Tambal stood there, two riders pulled away from the glittering line of people and animals and galloped up to him.

“In the name of the prince, our lord, we demand some of your fruit. His celestial highness is thirsty and has a desire for some of these strange apricots,” said an officer.

Tambal did not move, still numb from his recent experiences.

Now the prince himself came down from his carriage and said, "I am Jadugarzada, son of the magician-king of the East. Here is a bag of gold, oaf. I am having some of your fruit, because I am desirous of it. I am in a hurry to claim my bride, Princess Precious Pearl, daughter of Kahana, magician-king of the West."

At these words Tambal's heart turned over. But realizing that this must be the destiny which the sage had told him to follow, he offered the prince as much of the fruit as he could eat.

When the prince had eaten, he began to fall asleep. As he did so, horns, fur and huge ears started to grow out of him. When the soldiers shook him, the prince began to behave in a strange way. He claimed that he was normal, and that *they* were deformed.

The prince's councilors restrained him and held a hurried debate. Tambal claimed that all would have been well if the prince had not fallen asleep. Finally it was decided to put Tambal in the carriage and have him play the part of the prince. The horned Jadugarzada was tied to a horse with a veil thrown over his face, disguised as a servant woman.

"He may recover his wits eventually," said the councilors, "and, in any case, he is still our prince. Tambal shall marry the girl. Then, as soon as possible, we shall carry them all back to our own country for our king to solve the problem."

Tambal, biding his time and following his destiny, agreed to his own part in the masquerade.

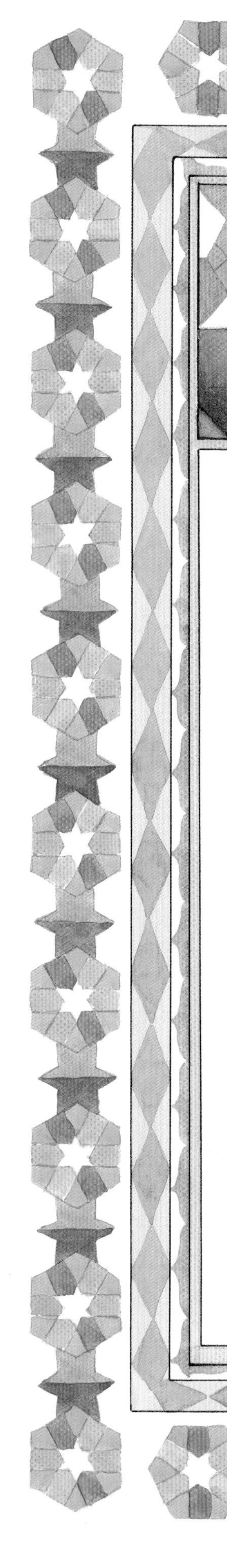

When the party arrived at the capital of the West, the king himself came out to meet them, and Tambal was taken to the princess as her bridegroom. She was so astonished that she nearly fainted, but Tambal whispered quickly what had happened. And so they were married, and the people had a great celebration.

In the meantime the horned prince had half recovered his wits, but not his human form, and his escort still kept him under cover. As soon as the feasting was over, the chief of the horned prince's party (who had been keeping Tambal and the princess under a very close watch) presented himself to the court. He said, "O Just and Glorious Monarch, Fountain of Wisdom, the time has now come, according to the pronouncements of our astrologers and soothsayers, to conduct the bridal pair back to our own land, so that they may be established in their new home under the most felicitous circumstances and influences."

The princess turned to Tambal in alarm, for she knew that as soon as they were on the open road, Jadugarzada would claim her and make an end of Tambal.

Tambal whispered to her, "Fear nothing. We must act as best we can, following our destiny. Agree to go, but say that you will not travel without the wooden horse."

At first the magician-king was annoyed at this wish of his daughter's. He realized that she wanted the horse because it was connected with her first suitor. But the chief minister of the horned prince said, "Majesty, this is just the desire for a toy, such as any young girl might have. Let her have her plaything so that we may make haste homeward."

So the magician-king agreed, and soon the splendid procession was on its way. After the king's escort had withdrawn, and before the party stopped for the night, the hideous Jadugarzada threw off his veil and cried out to Tambal, "Miserable author of my misfortunes! I will bind you hand and foot and take you back to my own land. Then you must tell me how to remove this enchantment, or I will have you flayed alive, inch by inch. Now, give me the Princess Precious Pearl!"

Tambal ran to the princess and, in front of the astonished party, rose into the sky on the wooden horse with Precious Pearl mounted behind him.

In minutes the couple alighted at the palace of King Mumkin. They related everything that had happened to them, and the king was almost overcome with delight at their safe return. He at once gave orders for the woodcarver to be released, rewarded, and applauded by all the citizens.

When King Mumkin was gathered to his fathers, Princess Precious Pearl and Prince Tambal succeeded him. Prince Hoshyar was pleased, too, because he was still entranced by the wondrous fish.

"I am glad for your own sakes, if you are happy," he said to them, "but I think there is nothing more rewarding than my work with the wondrous fish."

And this story is the origin of a strange saying among the people of that land, although they have forgotten its beginnings. The saying is: "Those who want fish can achieve much through fish, and those who do not know their heart's desire may first have to hear the story of the wooden horse."

Other Books by Idries Shah

For Young Readers
The Farmer's Wife
Neem the Half-Boy
The Lion Who Saw Himself in the Water
The Silly Chicken
The Boy Without A Name
The Clever Boy and the Terrible, Dangerous Animal
The Old Woman and the Eagle
The Man with Bad Manners
World Tales

Literature
The Hundred Tales of Wisdom
A Perfumed Scorpion
Caravan of Dreams
Wisdom of the Idiots
The Magic Monastery
The Dermis Probe

Novel
Kara Kush

Informal Beliefs
Oriental Magic
The Secret Lore of Magic

Humor
The Exploits of the Incomparable Mulla Nasrudin
The Pleasantries of the Incredible Mulla Nasrudin
The Subtleties of the Inimitable Mulla Nasrudin
The World of Nasrudin
Special Illumination

Travel
Destination Mecca

Human Thought
Learning How to Learn
The Elephant in the Dark
Thinkers of the East
Reflections
A Veiled Gazelle
Seeker After Truth

Sufi Studies
The Sufis
The Way of the Sufi
Tales of the Dervishes
The Book of the Book
Neglected Aspects of Sufi Study
The Commanding Self

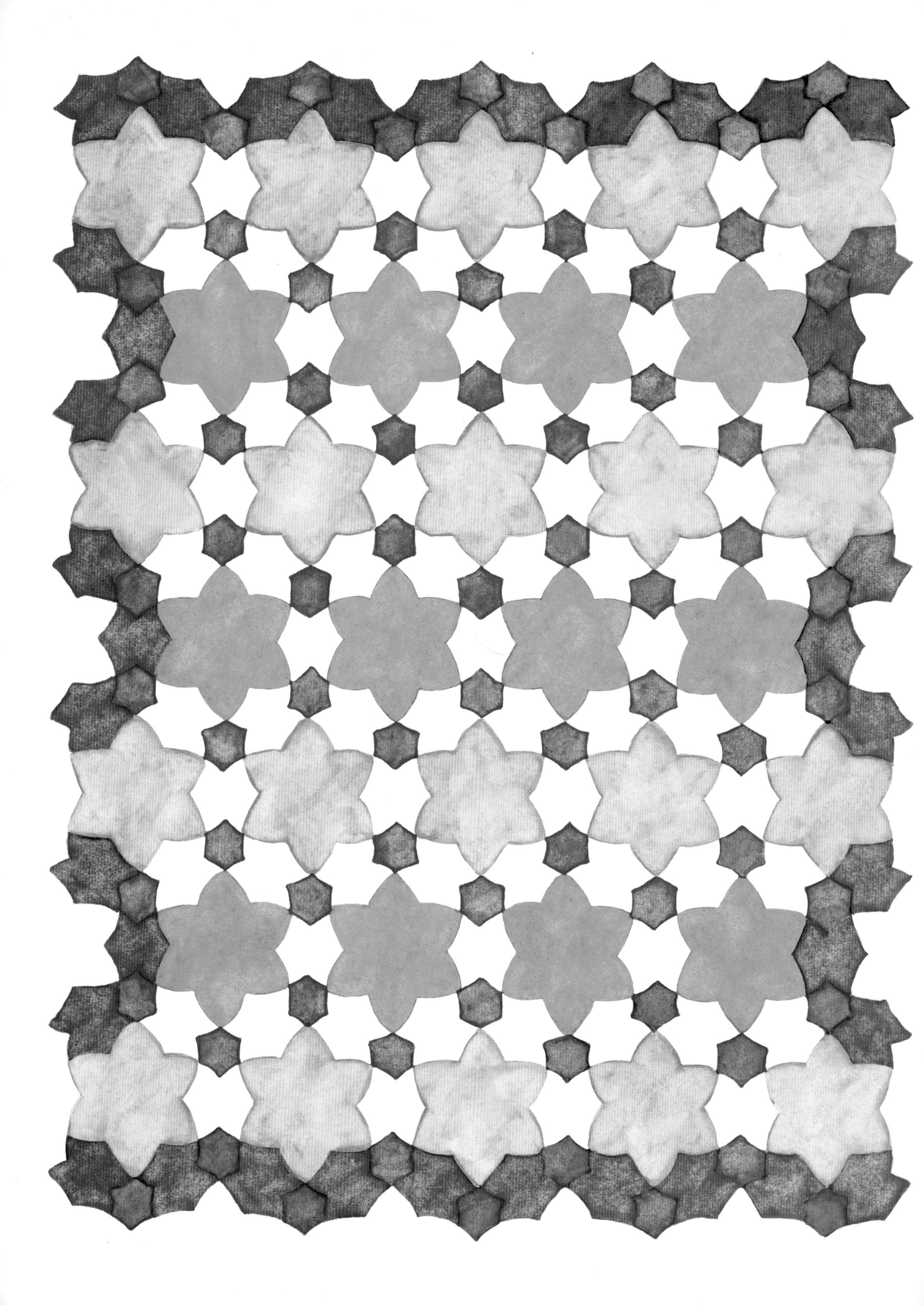